Inside the World of
HORSES

Christopher Rawson, Joanna Spector
and Elizabeth Polling

Illustrated by Eric Rowe,
Gordon King and Joan Thompson

Designed by Bob Scott

Consultant and contributor: Patricia Smyly

Contents

2   How Horses Began

4   Some Famous Breeds

6   Horse Transport

8   War Horses

10 Working Horses

12 Famous Show Jumpers

14 Great Show Jumping Events

16 Showing

18 Dressage

20 Eventing

22 Other Horse Sports

24 Racing Stables

26 At the Races

28 Lipizzaners

30 The Rodeo

32 Index

USBORNE

How Horses Began

The world of horses is a very exciting and interesting one. Although most working horses have now been replaced by cars, lorries and tractors, there are many different horse sports and still some jobs that only horses can do.

Horses are gentle, friendly animals. They are easy to teach if their training is done with patience, experience and lots of time. As well as being used for riding, horses are bred and trained as race horses, hunters and carriage horses. They are also taught to do difficult dressage movements, to be expert show jumpers, and to take part in displays.

Horses and ponies have a very long history. There were herds of horses roaming the world long before the first people, who lived about a million years ago. At that time horses looked quite different from modern ones.

At first men hunted the wild horses which lived in Asia and Europe for food. Later people began to use them to carry goods, food and weapons, and to ride them. Over the centuries, horses and ponies changed men's way of life. People could travel much farther and faster on horseback or in carts than on foot. Mounted warriors could easily defeat enemies on foot and farmers could grow bigger crops with horse-drawn ploughs and farm machinery. With careful selection and breeding for different jobs and sports, these useful animals have become the horses we know today.

Eohippus (The Dawn Horse)

The first pre-historic animals to be recognized as horses were timid little creatures. They lived in the woodlands of North America and Europe about 55 million years ago. They were about the size of a fox but looked like a small deer. Their colouring helped them to hide among the trees from large meat-eating animals. They could not bite off grass with their teeth so they lived on soft leaves and young plants. They had four toes on each front foot and three on each of their hind feet. Each toe had a small round hoof at the end. This was the main clue to the discovery that Eohippus was the first horse.

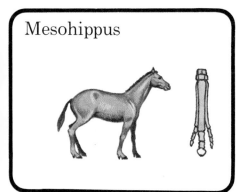

Mesohippus

After about 20 million years the Dawn horses had changed to look like this. They had grown a little taller and had three toes on each foot. They lived more in the open, ate grass, and could run faster.

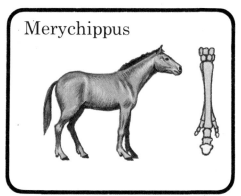

Merychippus

After millions of years, horses had become about 1 metre taller and lived on the open plains. They still had three toes on each foot but the centre one had grown larger and the side ones were smaller.

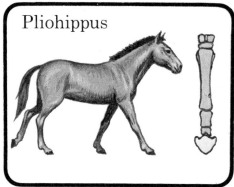

Pliohippus

The first true one-toed horses lived about five million years ago. By then they looked much more like modern horses. Pliohippus was also the ancient ancestor of the zebras and asses of today.

Domestication

Primitive men in Europe hunted horses for food for thousands of years. About 4,000 years ago, they began to capture them instead of killing them. The first people to tame horses were probably the tribesmen who roamed the treeless plains of Central Asia. They kept small herds of the tough little ponies which lived there for their meat, milk and skins. These people learned to harness the ponies so they could pull loads and they also began to ride them.

Southern Horse

Northern Horse

Two quite different types of horses developed in Europe and Asia. In Southern Europe they became fine-boned with smooth coats. They could run very fast and were like Arab horses of today.

Only much tougher ponies could live in the cooler weather of Northern Asia. They had thick skins and long, rough coats. They probably looked like this Przvalski, or wild Mongolian, horse.

Some Famous Breeds

There are now nearly 200 official breeds of horses and ponies in the world. They all came from the Northern or Southern types. Different breeds developed over millions of years, due to changes in the weather and the food where they lived. Horses that did not adapt to these changes died out. Only small, hardy ponies could survive in the cold, mountainous areas of Northern Europe. Larger, heavier types of horses lived in the warm, grassy lowlands. Light-boned, fast animals developed in the hot, dry regions of Southern Asia. Many years of careful matching and cross-breeding produced the horses we know today. On these pages are some of the horses that have been bred for a particular job or sport.

German Riding and Carriage Horses

Most of the German breeds, such as the Hanoverian shown here, were the result of crossing heavy Northern horses with fine English Thoroughbreds. One of the most popular breeds, the Trakhener, was bred from an English Thoroughbred, Perfectionist. These horses were used mainly for pulling carriages. Now they have become lighter and more elegant in build and are very good at dressage, show jumping and eventing. Another German breed, the Oldenberg, has become famous for driving events.

East European Horses

In Poland and Hungary horses developed in much the same way as in Germany but with more Arab horses used for cross-breeding. The Soviet Union has the biggest variety of horses because there are so many different types of country and weather inside its borders. Its ponies are very tough and hardy and are able to live on very little food. Many Russian horses are bred for trotting races, like this Akhal Teke horse.

American Horses

All the North American breeds were developed from European horses taken across the Atlantic by early settlers. The Tennessee Walking Horse, shown here, was used by farmers in the South. Their special running walk gave a smooth ride. The lively Criollo ponies of South America, used for herding cattle, developed from the horses brought by the Spanish who invaded Mexico in the 16th century.

Southern European Horses

Very attractive and popular types of horses live in Southern Europe. They usually have short legs, deep bodies and grey coats. They include the Andalusian horses of Spain and Portugal, shown here, the famous Lipizzaners, and the Camargue ponies of Southern France. They are all closely related to the old Barb horses which were probably brought to Spain by Arab invaders. These horses are especially good at the high-school work which became fashionable in Vienna in the 17th century and has been carried on ever since.

English Thoroughbreds

These noble horses are the result of cross-breeding native British ponies of the Northern type with Barb, Turk and Arabian horses of the Southern type. The Thoroughbred has been developed into a perfect racing animal. It is also an excellent riding horse with good proportions and natural balance. They make good hunters and jumpers when crossed with part-Thoroughbred or part-Arab horses.

Heavy Horses

The mild weather and lush grass in France, Holland and Germany helped to develop the heavy horses. They are a much larger and stronger type of the Northern horse and were produced by carefully breeding the largest animals. They were once war horses and used as chargers by French knights. Modern French breeds include the Percheron and Breton. In Britain heavy horses like these Shire horses were used for all farm work. Other breeds such as Suffolk Punches and Clydesdales are still very popular.

Horse Transport

Horses have been used to pull wagons and carriages for thousands of years. One of the oldest ever found was the state chariot of Egypt's boy king, Tutankhamen, who lived over 3,000 years ago. Until the beginning of this century, when motor cars took over, the only way to travel fast or move heavy loads overland was to use horses.

Coaching

The mail and passenger coaches in the 18th century were the fastest and most comfortable ever built. They were better made than other wagons and carriages and their improved suspension gave travellers a smoother ride. There were good stopping places about every 24km along the coach roads, where the teams of four horses were changed. The tired horses were left there and fresh ones pulled the coaches to the next stopping place. Coach horses were chosen for their speed and strength. But the work was so hard that coach horses could rarely be used for more than about three years. Coaches like this carried passengers all over Europe.

Coaching

Chariot

Greek war chariots, like this one, were used in battle until about 700 BC. After that, they were used for hunting and chariot races. These were exciting but dangerous.

Farm Cart

This type of farm wagon was used from the 14th century onwards. It could be pulled by several horses in a line. The traces and much of the harness were made of rope.

European Chaise

Fashionable and rich gentlemen took up driving as a sport late in the 18th century. They drove this type of light two-wheeled cart in towns and on their country estates.

Parts of a Harness

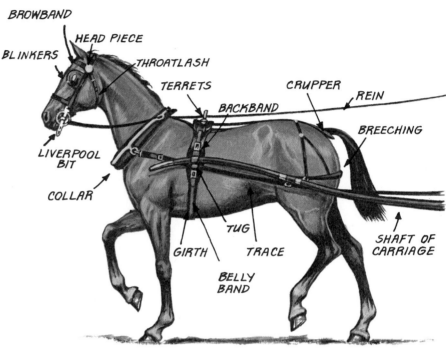

Driving harness may look complicated, but each part is carefully made to let the horse pull comfortably and give the driver maximum control. Most important is the collar, which should fit perfectly, and the traces, with which the horse pulls the vehicle. Tugs on the backband support the shafts which stop the vehicle from tipping. The breeching fits round the hindquarters and is attached to the shafts or the traces to hold the vehicle back on steep hills or when slowing down.

Covered Wagon

Settlers travelling to the West of America had carts, called Praïrie Schooners, like this one. They were pulled by horses or oxen and carried all the family possessions.

Charabanc

This is what a coach party looked like about a hundred years ago. The vehicle was called a charabanc and was used on large country estates to carry members of shooting parties, or the servants and guns. Later charabancs were used for public sight-seeing tours.

War Horses

Horses have probably been used in war since men first learned to ride them. The Assyrians had mounted bowmen in about 900 BC. They must have trained their horses well because the bowmen needed both hands to shoot. Since then and until the beginning of the 20th century, mounted soldiers have been an important part of armies. Horses were also used to carry baggage, food and weapons, and to pull cannons and heavy guns.

1 Romans

The Roman cavalry, who wore metal armour, needed strong horses to carry the extra weight. A special breed was developed for them. The Romans did not have saddles or stirrups so they had to grip their horses with their thighs and could carry only light weapons. They were armed with a spear, a shield and a short sword.

2 Tartars

These fierce horsemen, led by Ghenghis Khan, conquered land from the China Sea to the Baltic Sea in the 13th century. They could travel up to 128 km a day on their tough Mongolian ponies. The Tartars even ate and slept on horseback. They were the first to use snaffle bridles, and saddles with stirrups.

3 Knights of the Middle Ages

These soldiers rode into battle on huge horses, called destriers. By the 13th century both the men and their horses had become too heavily armoured. Slow and clumsy, they were easily defeated by bowmen in such battles as Crecy and Agincourt between the French and English.

4 Cavalry Regiments

Cavalry again became the strongest attacking force in most armies in the 17th, 18th and 19th centuries. Many of the great battles in Europe were won by famous cavalry commanders, such as Charles II of Sweden, Frederick the Great of Prussia, Napoleon of France and Marlborough and Wellington of England.

Frederick the Great was the first commander to understand the importance of good feed and proper training for cavalry horses. He also provided extra horses, called remounts, for soldiers whose horses were killed or injured in action. He introduced horse artillery to the battlefield. Six horses, in pairs, pulled the heavy fields guns. These were fired at the enemy before the cavalry charged them.

Here the British and French cavalry are in action at the Battle of Waterloo in 1815. French soldiers charged at the trot while the British galloped into battle.

The two most famous chargers at this time were Napoleon's grey Arab stallion, called Marengo, and Wellington's chestnut stallion, called Copenhagen.

5 The 20th Century

By the beginning of the First World War, which started in 1914, machine guns which could fire up to 800 bullets a minute, field guns which fired high-explosive shells, and quick-firing rifles had all been invented. Horses could not be protected from these weapons and the cavalry were often replaced by tanks and armoured cars. The last big cavalry charge was at Musino, near Moscow, during the Second World War. In ten minutes, 2,000 Russian mounted soldiers were killed by German guns.

Cavalry is no longer used by armies today but most countries still have some mounted soldiers for state and official ceremonies.

Working Horses

When men began to farm instead of only hunting for food many thousands of years ago, they first found a use for horses instead of just killing them to eat. Until the middle of the 19th century, horses still did much of the heavy work for farmers and pulled many different sorts of carts and wagons. Some are still used today for work that machines cannot do. Here are some of the jobs that horses did in the past and still do.

19th Century

One of the most exciting jobs for horses was pulling the heavy, steam fire engines in the 19th century. This American 'steamer' is rushing to a fire at full gallop. The man at the back of the engine is the 'stoker'. He is trying to get up enough steam to work the powerful water pumps as soon as they reach the fire. These horses were especially selected for their speed and strength.

Draught Horses

Heavy draught horses, such as the Percheron, Jutland or these Shire horses, were first bred to carry knights in armour into battle. They were so strong, they were soon being used to pull the ploughs on farms and heavy barges on the canals. They were also used on roads to draw heavy loads, such as timber and coal. Most of this work is now done by powerful lorries but heavy horses are still kept by some breweries to deliver beer in the city centres.

These horses are pulling a beer dray. It is a low, open-sided wagon. The barrels are stacked on top of the dray and sometimes also slung underneath.

Shrimp Fishers

This unusual type of work for horses can be seen on the Belgian coast. Placid and solidly-built Breton horses drag trawl nets through the shallow water to catch shrimps.

Horses are still very useful in other areas, such as mountains. High in the Austrian Tyrol, pretty chestnut Haflinger ponies pull felled trees over rough ground that is too steep for machines. Hardy Fjord ponies in Scandinavia do the same sort of work.

Ranching

In America, Australia and New Zealand horses are widely used on ranches. Most of their work is herding cattle or sheep from one pasture to another. Some breeds, such as the American Quarterhorse, are trained to 'cut', or single out, one animal from the herd, and help the rider when he ropes it.

Pit Ponies

There were over 70,000 pit ponies working in Britain's coal mines in 1900. Now there are only about 100 left. Tough native breeds, such as Shetland, Welsh and Fell ponies, pulled the tubs of coal on tracks along the narrow passages. They lived underground from the age of about four until too old to work.

Famous Show Jumpers in Action

Show jumping looks an exciting way of life if you watch famous riders at a show or on television. But to become a top-class rider needs a lot of hard work and training. Show jumpers have to be totally dedicated and spend most of their lives riding and training their horses. They also have to find and train young horses for the future years. But for the few who do succeed, the rewards are great. Here are some who have become famous through skill and determination.

Hartwig Steenken

This very talented rider is seen here on Kosmos. But most of Steenken's successes were with the Hanoverian mare called Simona. With her he won the 1974 World title and rode in the winning team at the Munich Olympics.

Eddie Macken

One of Ireland's most outstanding young riders, he has won most of the top awards in Europe on Boomerang pictured here. Macken finished second to Hartwig Steenken in the 1974 World Championship, riding Pele.

Harvey Smith

Seen here on the German horse, Salvador, Harvey Smith is one of the great personalities of show jumping. He bought his first horse for £40 and was soon asked to join the British team. He rode in the Mexico and Munich Olympics, and has won five British Grands Prix.

Behind the Scenes

Grooms travel with the horses to show jumping events to look after them. There are wooden stables at most big shows.

Preparing the horses for jumping must be done with great care. This groom is putting on tendon boots to protect the horse's legs.

If the ground is soft or the horse may have to turn sharply, metal studs are screwed into his shoes to stop him slipping.

A rider needs time to get ready before jumping. She must wear the right number. This rider is buckling on her spurs.

Alwin Schockemöhle

This popular German rider won the individual gold medal in the Montreal Olympics in 1976 riding Warwick. He has been German national champion three times and is here riding Rex the Robber.

David Broome

One of Britain's most stylish riders, Broome is able to coax the best out of any horse. Here he is riding Red 'A'. He has won two Olympic bronze medals, the 1970 World title and three European titles.

Rodney Jenkins

The most successful American show jumper, here riding Number One Spy, he has won a huge number of championships. His most famous horse is the gelding, Idle Dice.

Some horses have to be 'warmed-up' in the practice area for a long time. Others need only one or two practice jumps.

All the tack must be checked before the event. This horse is having his bit adjusted and the girth may be tightened.

While waiting for his turn, a rider will walk his horse round. He may keep the rugs on until the last minute if it is cold.

After the horse has jumped, the groom gives him a tit-bit and puts on his rugs. He will loosen the girth and walk the horse until cool.

Great Show Jumping Events

Show jumping is a very expert sport, with valuable prizes to be won at all the important events. But there are still some special competitions, such as the Olympic Games, which all riders hope to win regardless of the prize money. The winners of these sorts of competitions have reached the top of their sport. Riders who earn their living by riding are called professionals. All others are called amateurs.

Olympic Games

The Olympic gold, silver and bronze medals are the most highly valued awards in show jumping. The Games take place every four years. Many riders spend the years in between them preparing their horses. Only amateur riders may take part which means that some well-known professional riders cannot compete. This might make the medals seem easier to win but competition is always keen. Alwin Schockemöhle's winning performance at the Montreal Olympics was outstanding. Here he is riding Warwick Rex. He was the only entrant to jump all the fences twice without a fault. It was one of the most difficult Olympic courses ever built.

Individual Grand Prix Olympic Games 1976

A course builder has to think of many things when he is designing a course. He tries to set the competitors as many different problems as possible. So he builds a course with a variety of jumps, with different turns and distances between them. The course should test the rider by making him work out how to ride it. It tests the horse for obedience, suppleness and jumping ability. This was the course for the first round in the 1976 Olympics.

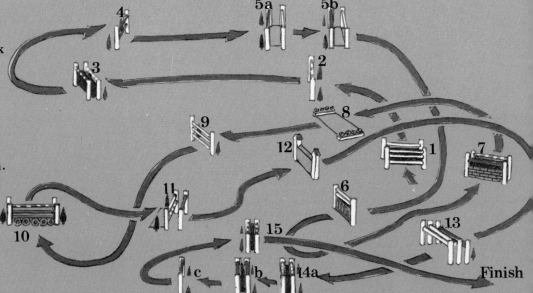

World Championship

This is also held every four years, between the Olympics. It is open to amateur and professional riders. It is usually held in the country of the rider who last won the Championship. This event is a great test of horsemanship because the best four riders have to ride each others horses. This means that the rider with the most difficult horse often wins. Hartwig Steenken on Simona (left) won in 1974.

British Jumping Derby

This event is held at Hickstead in Great Britain every year. It is different from other competitions because natural obstacles, such as banks, hedges and ditches, are included in the course.

It is also very long and difficult. It needs great concentration and strength by horses and riders. One feature of the course is the Derby Bank. Here Judy Crago on Bouncer shows how to

come down the Bank by sliding from the top and jumping off about two-thirds of the way down. They finished equal second in 1976. The winner was Eddie Macken on Boomerang.

European Championships

This is quite a simple type of competition. It usually has two rounds with the scores from each round added together. If any riders then have equal scores, they jump again and the fastest one with the fewest faults wins. The Championship takes place every two years and, until 1973, there were separate ones for men and women. The winner that year was Paddy McMahon of Great Britain on Pennwood Forge Mill (above).

Problem Fences

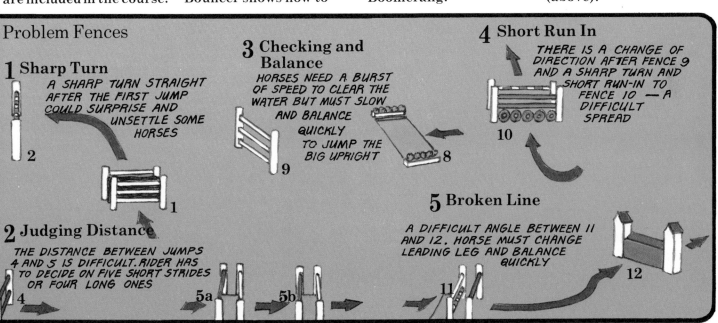

1 Sharp Turn
A SHARP TURN STRAIGHT AFTER THE FIRST JUMP COULD SURPRISE AND UNSETTLE SOME HORSES

2 Judging Distance
THE DISTANCE BETWEEN JUMPS 4 AND 5 IS DIFFICULT. RIDER HAS TO DECIDE ON FIVE SHORT STRIDES OR FOUR LONG ONES

3 Checking and Balance
HORSES NEED A BURST OF SPEED TO CLEAR THE WATER BUT MUST SLOW AND BALANCE QUICKLY TO JUMP THE BIG UPRIGHT

4 Short Run In
THERE IS A CHANGE OF DIRECTION AFTER FENCE 9 AND A SHARP TURN AND SHORT RUN-IN TO FENCE 10 — A DIFFICULT SPREAD

5 Broken Line
A DIFFICULT ANGLE BETWEEN 11 AND 12. HORSE MUST CHANGE LEADING LEG AND BALANCE QUICKLY

Showing

Show classes for horses and ponies are held at most local and international horse shows. Anyone with a suitable horse or pony can take part. The essentials are that a horse has good conformation—that is, a good shape—straight action and 'clean' or undamaged legs. He must also be well-mannered and schooled. There are classes for all types of horses and ponies. Most are ridden but some are 'in hand' or led. Other classes are combined with performance, such as dressage or jumping.

Child's Ridden Pony

Private Driving

Private Driving

Driving for pleasure is becoming a popular hobby. Many shows now hold special driving classes for private 'turnouts'. The pony must be correctly harnessed and the vehicle smartly painted. A judge looks for good action and responses from the pony. The most exciting horses to watch in harness are Hackneys. With their high, graceful stepping action, they seem to float over the ground.

Child's Ridden Pony

These classes are usually divided into three parts; for ponies up to 12.2, 13.2 and 14.2 hands, ridden by children up to 12, 14 and 16 years old. The judge looks for an attractive 'well-made' pony which moves nicely and is well schooled. He must have good manners and be safe, obedient and trustworthy.

Arabs

Arabs

Arab horses are usually shown 'in-hand', or led, with mane and tail flowing, never plaited. There are also ridden and performance classes for them. Points the judges look for include a small head, a short back, sloping shoulders and free but straight leg action. All Arabs must be pure-bred and registered.

Preparing to Show

1 There is lots of hard work to be done before a show. All the tack must be spotlessly clean with the bit and stirrups polished.

2 The final grooming will be done on the morning of the show. This may include washing any white leg markings.

3 Next comes plaiting. This must be done very neatly. Sections of mane are plaited, folded under and sewn into place.

4 Horses sometimes become excited before a class. Twenty minutes on the lunge often helps them relax and warm up quietly.

16

Cobs

Cobs are small, stocky horses of not more than 15.3 hands, and of no particular breed. They were first bred as riding horses for heavy or elderly riders and must be very well behaved. In cob, hunter and hack classes, the riders dismount to allow the judge to put their horses through their paces himself. The judge may then see the horse unsaddled and have him led to watch his action and overall appearance.

Hunters

Hunters are generally divided into classes by the weight they can carry when hunting. They must be strong, obedient and have a good galloping action.

Hacks

These are elegant riding horses that must have nearly perfect conformation and manners. There are often Ladies Hack classes which are ridden side-saddle.

In the Ring

At the first line-up the best horses come out in turn to give a short, individual show, which the riders plan beforehand.

The judge may then want to look at the horses more closely. The saddles are taken off so he can judge the overall shape.

He will then ask to see each horse trotted up in-hand. He can then tell if the action is straight or there is a fault.

The horses are remounted and the judge makes his final decision. They are called into line for the presentations.

Dressage

Dressage is quite simply the training of a horse for riding. It can be used just to make him more obedient and comfortable to ride, or to get him ready for other things like show jumping. But dressage in its purest form goes a lot further than that. It prepares the horse for exacting tests of obedience and movement. The main object is to show that he can move lightly and freely while carrying a rider and willingly obey commands.

Everything should look natural and easy, with the rider's aids, or signals, almost invisible.

Dressage competitions are held at many levels, from preliminary to advanced, and then there are special classes such as Prix St Georges and Grand Prix. Three judges mark each movement separately and their marks are then added together. Here are some famous dressage horses and riders in action.

Piaffe
This is one of the most difficult movements in an advanced test. It is a slow trot, on the spot. The horse springs from one front leg and opposite hind leg to the other opposite legs as if he were moving forward. It is a test of balance, strength and control.

Reiner Klimke
Dr Reiner Klimke and his horse, Mehmed, were one of West Germany's top dressage partnerships. They won the World championship in 1974 and were bronze medallists at the Montreal Olympics. Here they are making a change of tempo, or pace, from working trot to collected trot. Even small changes in tempo have to be shown clearly and made at exactly the right place. This has to be done without upsetting the horse's balance or rhythm.

Christine Stückelberger

This young rider from Switzerland reached the top of her sport when she won the gold medal at the Montreal Olympics in 1976. Here she is riding Granat, a big German-bred Holstein horse, in Vienna. They are performing a collected trot. Christine started riding at the age of 13 when an aunt paid for some lessons as a present. Since then she has been Swiss champion six times. She is trained by Georg Wahl, a pupil of the Spanish Riding School.

Pirouette

This tests the suppleness of the horse's spine and his balance. He turns a complete circle on the spot in a collected canter. He keeps all four feet moving in the canter sequence. The hind feet step almost in the same spot. The front legs step in a circle round them.

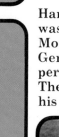

Harry Boldt

Harry Boldt on Woycheck was a runner-up in Montreal for West Germany. Here they are performing a pirouette. The horse's weight is over his inside hind leg.

Tonny Jensen

This is Tonny Jensen of Denmark riding Fox. He is just finishing a series of changes of leg at the canter.

Dominique d'Esme

Dominique d'Esme is one of France's most successful dressage riders. Here she is riding Carioca II in an extended trot. The extended paces are most difficult as the horse must have a very strong back and hindquarters. This pace is not faster than the others but the strides are longer and lower.

Jennie Loriston-Clarke

Jennie Loriston-Clarke is one of Britain's top dressage riders. Here she is competing on Kadett in the Munich Olympic Games. The horse is performing a collected canter down the centre of the arena. In movements like this, the horse has to move in a perfectly straight line, just as a circle must be ridden perfectly round.

19

Eventing

This is one of the hardest and most exciting horse sports. Major events last for three days. They test riders and their horses in three ways. Dressage tests a horse's obedience and control. Cross-country tests his strength, fitness and agility. Show jumping tests that he is still fit and able to jump accurately even when he is tired after the long cross-country part.

The idea for this competition came from the army. Cavalry horses had to be obedient, able to gallop across country, jump anything and work again the next day. Event horses need years of training before they are ready to take part in top class events.

1 Dressage

The dressage test is on the first day. It shows if a horse is obedient to the rider and if the rider is giving the right signals to the horse. The judges look for a supple horse that moves obediently and is calm and has an even rhythm in all paces. All the different movements of the test, which may last for up to ten minutes, have to be learned by heart. It is very hard for the horse because he is so fit and ready to gallop a long way next day. He has to concentrate very hard on the slow and exact paces in the small dressage arena.

Lucinda Prior-Palmer and Be Fair of Britain in the dressage test at Lühmuhlen in Germany. She won the European Championship in 1975 and in 1977.

Behind the Scenes

Walking the course is essential. Riders look at the fences and test the ground for firmness, even if it is under water.

2 Cross-Country

This is the most exciting day of the competition. There are four parts with two sections of Roads and Tracks. A horse can walk and trot along the route, and gallop the Steeplechase course. The final part is the cross-country. This is the real test of courage, skill and strength. The course may be up to 6 km long with lots of difficult jumps and natural obstacles, such as walls, banks and water.

Herbert Bloecker rides Albrant in the cross-country course at Lümuhlen. They were members of Germany's silver medal-winning team at the Montreal Olympics.

The horse's legs are often protected with bandages or boots. Thick grease helps him to slide over a fence if he hits it.

The roads and tracks phase is the longest. The horses can walk part of the way and cool down before the cross-country.

On the steeplechase phase, the time limit is very short. Horses gallop round the course which has wide brush fences.

The ten-minute break before the cross-country allows horses and riders to relax and cool off. Some horses are washed all over.

Horst Karsten of West Germany riding Sioux, makes a spectacular leap during the cross-country phase of the Munich Olympics. They were members of the team which won the bronze medal.

Bruce Davidson of the U.S.A. rides Plain Sailing (right) at the Munich Olympics. He became the World Three-Day-Event Champion in 1974.

Richard Meade rides Wayfarer through a combination fence at Crookham in Britain. He was a member of the British gold medal-winning team in the Mexico Olympics.

3 Showjumping

The final test comes after a hard day of galloping and jumping. The horse must still be fit enough to twist and turn his way round a show jumping course without knocking down any of the fences.

Princess Anne is here riding Doublet in the show jumping at Badminton in Britain. They won the European Championship in 1972 and were in the winning British team.

6 All riders have to weigh in and out to ensure they are carrying the right weight. Light riders need extra lead-filled saddle cloths.

7 After the cross-country phase, a horse is checked for injuries. A sweat rug is put on him and he is walked until quite cool.

8 On the morning of the final day, vets inspect all horses. If a horse is lame or weak, he cannot compete in the jumping.

9 Although the show jumps may look easy, horses are stiff and may be careless. They are warmed up for some time before jumping.

Other Horse Sports

There are many exciting horse sports and games. Some of them probably began soon after men first learned to ride and drive horses. Hunting and polo are many centuries old. Others, such as combined driving, are quite new. Hunting and steeple-chasing have only become really popular since people have had the time to learn about horses and enjoy them.

Trotting

Trotting has developed from the ancient and very dangerous sport of chariot racing. Now breeding and training horses specially for trotting is an important business in many countries. The horses race round special tracks pulling light carriages called gigs or sulkies. A competitor in a trotting race is eliminated if his horse breaks into a canter. There are two types of trotting horses. The true trotter moves diagonally with near fore and off hind legs together. The pacer moves laterally with near fore and near hind legs together.

Scurry Driving

One of the newest types of driving competition, scurry driving is enormous fun to do or watch. A twisty course is set out in the arena, with pairs of markers, like these, set an exact distance apart. The aim is to complete the course as fast as possible, passing between the markers without touching them. The driver is allowed one passenger who can lean out at sharp corners to help balance the carriage.

Combined Driving

This competition is for teams of four horses pulling light four-wheeled carriages. It is rather like three-day eventing as it has three sections to test the driver's skills and the fitness and training of the horses. The first section is for presentation and dressage. The second is the exciting cross-country phase, with lots of hazards, as our picture shows. Finally there is an obstacle test, like the scurry driving.

Hunting

This popular sport is a good way of training for horses and riders. They learn to ride through woods and across open country at different paces, and to jump hedges, walls, banks, streams and ditches.

Steeplechasing

These exciting races, like the famous Grand National, started in the 18th century when country gentlemen challenged each other to races from one church steeple to the next, jumping the hedges in between.

Polo

Polo is one of the oldest horse sports. There are records of a similar game being played in Persia more than 2,000 years ago. The rules have changed little since then. Two teams of four riders each try to score goals by hitting a small ash or bamboo ball, only 83mm across, between two posts. The pitch is 274 metres long and 146 metres wide. In Europe, a game has six periods of play, called chukkas, each lasting seven minutes. Polo ponies are about 15.1 hands and are specially bred for speed and to be able to turn and stop quickly.

Racing Stables

Racing stables are interesting and exciting places to work, especially before a big race for one of their horses. All race horse owners hope that their horses will win races and valuable prizes. They send them to racing stables where they are carefully looked after and trained. Stables are owned by the trainer who is in charge of all the horses. He decides what sort of races are most suitable for each horse. He also plans a training programme to increase the speed and strength of each horse and make them as fit as possible for racing.

Most stable work and exercise is done by men and girls, called 'lads', who work for the trainer and may be hoping to become jockeys later. There is also a head lad who makes sure the trainer's orders are carried out. A travelling head lad is in charge of the horses on race days.

The Stable Yard

Race horses live in stables, called boxes, which surround a stable yard. The stables are large and solidly-built to be as warm and draught-free as possible. Beds of straw or wood shavings lie deep on the floor and are banked up round the walls to stop the horses from injuring themselves. The tack room, feed store and muck heap are all close to the boxes. Racing stables are busiest in the morning when all the horses, except any which are ill or have been injured, are ridden out. Usually the stable lads exercise

A Day's Training

1 Morning Feed

The head lad is up first, at about 5 a.m., to check each horse and see that all is well. He then prepares the morning feeds which are given to the horses after watering. They are then left in peace and quiet to eat and digest their food.

2 Tacked Up

The lads come on duty at about 6.30 a.m., to muck-out and brush over their first horses. Horses are then tacked-up, usually in a snaffle bridle and exercise saddle. On cold mornings they may wear a short 'quarter' sheet to keep them warm.

3 On the Gallops

The first 'lot' of horses will go out for work at first light. The lads are 'legged-up' and walk round until everyone is ready. Horses then file out in a 'string', the older ones leading. The trainer may ride with them or meet them on the gallops to watch them work. The gallops are well cared-for stretches of grass, sand or wood shavings which can be used all year round. Horses do most of their work at canter to condition their muscles, heart and lungs. They progress to 'fast work' and then to short gallops.

5 Evening Stables

Before the horses are rugged-up and given their last feeds the trainer makes an inspection. He notes the horse's condition and looks for signs of injury or strain. He may suggest that the head lad changes the horse's food.

4 Strapping

the horses. Sometimes they are ridden by the jockeys who want to get to know the horses before they ride them in a race. As well as exercising the horses, there are lots of ordinary stable jobs for the lads to do. They clean the tack, fill haynets, clean the yard and prepare the feeds. Fit race horses may need four or five feeds a day. The blacksmith visits the stables regularly to look after the horses' feet. The vet comes to examine and treat any sick horses. The afternoons are usually rest times for the horses and lads.

At about 4 p.m. the evening stable routine begins. The boxes are cleaned out and the horses given hay and water. The lad then 'straps' the horse. This is a very thorough grooming that includes massage to tone up the muscles and circulation.

Trainer's Instructions

This string of horses is on the gallops. They file around the trainer who gives instructions for each horse.

Working Upsides

A young horse may work 'upsides' an older one. This gets him used to the idea of other horses around him and encourages him to race.

At the Races

Speed contests between horses have probably been held since horses were domesticated by men. The ancient Greeks held races over 2,500 years ago but these were soon replaced by chariot racing. There are now two main sorts of racing; flat racing with no obstacles, and steeplechasing where the horses jump fences at speed. Flat racing is a summer sport when the ground is hard. The courses are short. Steeplechasing takes place in the winter when the ground is soft. The courses are longer and the horses are trained for stamina and jumping.

1 Racecourse Stables

Horses arrive early at the racecourse so they can recover from their journeys by horsebox. They are strictly guarded. Only the lads and trainers are allowed to visit them. The horses are not fed or watered for up to four hours before a race.

2 Saddling Up

Each jockey is carefully weighed, holding his saddle, before a race. The trainer then takes the saddle to a special saddling box near the paddock. The horses are taken there about 20 minutes before the race. They are saddled-up and led down to the paddock.

3 In the Paddock

Stable lads lead the horses around the parade ring in the paddock. This gives the people at the races a chance to watch the horses walking round and to decide which one they think will win. The owners of the horses and the trainers wait in the middle of the paddock for the jockeys to arrive. In this picture the signal has just been given for the jockeys to mount. The horses' rugs are taken off and their girths tightened. When all the jockeys have mounted, they go out on to the race track.

4 The Start

This is the start of a flat race. Helpers have led the horses into the stalls from the back. Sometimes horses will not go in willingly. The helpers have to push them from behind or even blindfold them. The starter then climbs on to his platform and raises his flag. Now the horses are 'under starter's orders'. Then he lowers his flag and presses a button to open the front gates of the stalls. "They're off."

5 The Finish

When several horses finish almost at the same time, it is called a close finish. Sometimes the finish is so close that the judge cannot decide which horse has won. Most race-courses have special photo-finish cameras which take pictures of the horses from both sides of the course as they gallop across the finishing line. Then the judge looks at the photographs and announces which horse has won.

6 Winners' Enclosure

Immediately after the race, the horses which have come first, second and third go back to the winners' enclosure. The jockeys dismount and take their saddles to the weighing room. The lads put sweat rugs over the horses and allow them to walk round and cool down. If there is a cup for winning the race, it will be presented to the owner.

7 Weighed In

Here is the winning jockey being 'weighed-in' by the Clerk of the Scales. This is to check that the jockeys and their saddles still weigh the same as before the race.

Lipizzaners

The pure white Lipizzaner horses of the Spanish Riding School at Vienna are one of the most beautiful and famous breeds in the world. They were first trained to be expert at high-school movements over 400 years ago, and have always been valuable and sought-after riding horses. Their great strength and light, graceful action made them the most popular horses in Europe for many centuries. Lipizzaners were originally bred in Spain by crossing Arab and Barb stallions with the native horses. Breeding continued only in the royal studs of Germany and Denmark, and at the Italian Imperial Stud at Lipizza where the most progress was made. The Spanish School was built in Vienna in 1735 and the Lipizzaners have performed there ever since, except during the First World War. Then the breeding stock was almost destroyed but a small herd was saved and returned to their home at Piber.

This is the Grand Hall of the Spanish Riding School in Vienna. It was once a royal ballroom. Beautifully decorated, it is lit by huge crystal chandeliers. These eight Lipizzaner stallions are performing a traditional quadrille. It ends with a movement called Crosswise Shifts. Each horse crosses the path of another very closely but without changing the rhythm of their paces.

Mares and Foals at Piber

All the horses for the Spanish School are bred at the Austrian National Stud Farm at Piber, high in the mountains. The foals are always dark brown or dark grey when they are born. They become whiter as they grow older, although a few foals stay dark. They leave their mothers at six months. The colts and fillies are separated when one year old. Their real schooling begins when they are over three.

Lipizzaner Brands

LINE	SIRE	DAM
PLUTO	P	
CONVERSANO	C	
NEAPOLITANO	N	
FAVORY	F	
MAETOSO	M	
SIGLAVY	S	

Lipizzaners have several brand marks to identify them. At first the horses bred at Lipizza in Italy had an 'L' brand on their left cheek. Now only horses from Piber have this mark. They also have a 'P' with a crown on their left hindquarters. These letters and signs show the horse's line or family. There are six stallion lines.

Education

Young stallions are broken with great care because they are not fully grown until they are seven years old. But they often go on working until they are over 25. Training begins at four. The horses are worked on the lungeing rein and in long-reins, like this. It helps to develop their balance and carriage —the way they move and hold themselves. Then the trainer starts riding but never for more than 45 minutes a day. He teaches the horse the rider's aids, or signals, and how to increase its forward speed. Training then becomes harder with turns, sideways movements and changes of pace.

Airs Above the Ground

Only some horses at the School become good enough to be taught 'airs above the ground'. These are spectacular rises and leaps. They were first used in battle so a horse could protect his rider by raising his front legs or leaping away from an enemy, kicking back at the same time.

The horses must first be able to perform high-school work on the ground, such as Pirouette, Piaffe and Passage. It is then decided if they are able to learn to work 'above the ground'. Their hind legs have to take all the weight off their front legs for several seconds. And a horse must be so strong and active that if he is prevented from moving forward, he rises into a Pesade, like the bay horse.

The horse in the lower picture is performing a Levade. This is a crouching rise. Other 'airs above the ground' are the Croupade, where the horse leaps forward from a Levade, and the Courbette. This is a series of forward leaps with all four legs off the ground. There are two types of jump. In the Ballotade the horse's body is level and his hind legs are slightly stretched out. The hind legs are fully stretched back for the Capriole. All the movements are done with great precision and power.

The Rodeo

At Rodeos cowboys show how good they are at riding and rounding up cattle. They can also win big prizes for other dangerous sports such as steer wrestling and bull riding.

Rodeos started about 100 years ago in the American West. After rounding up the cattle, the cowboys from several ranches would meet to have some fun. They took it in turns to show how they could rope a steer or stay on an untamed horse. The cattle were rounded up each year. Some were sold and the calves were branded with their owner's mark.

THE RIDER WAVES HIS FREE HAND IN THE AIR TO TRY AND KEEP HIS BALANCE. HE WILL LOSE MARKS IF HE TOUCHES ANY PART OF HIS HORSE.

Bareback Bronco Riding

In this competition a cowboy tries to balance on the back of a bucking horse for at least eight seconds. He has no saddle and only a loop of leather to hold on to. If he can jab the horse above its shoulders with his blunt spurs, he is awarded extra points by the judges.

HORSES ARE KEPT IN SMALL WOODEN PENS BESIDE THE ARENA, CALLED BUCKING PENS. COWBOYS DO NOT KNOW WHICH HORSE THEY WILL RIDE UNTIL JUST BEFORE THEIR TURN COMES.

1 Roping a Calf

2

Cowboys on round-ups have to rope calves and drag them to the branding fire. This event is a race against time to rope a calf and tie up three of its legs. First the calf is let out of its pen and then the cowboy rides out of his. The cowboy throws his rope to lasso the calf.

Roping horses are trained to stop immediately they see that the calf has been lassoed. The end of the rope is tied to the saddle horn. The cowboy leaps from his horse and runs to the calf while the horse pulls back all the time to keep the rope taut.

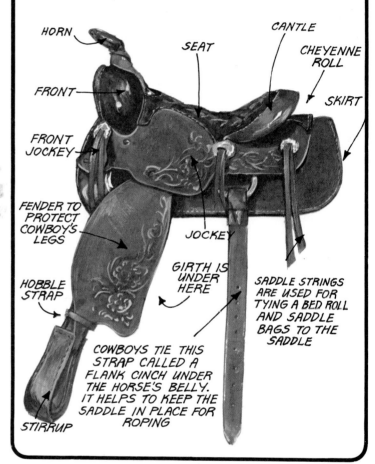

A Western Saddle

Cowboys sometimes spend all day on horseback so their saddles must be very comfortable. They also have to be strong enough to hold a fighting steer tied to the saddle horn after the cowboy has lassoed it.

HORN

FRONT

FRONT JOCKEY

FENDER TO PROTECT COWBOY'S LEGS

HOBBLE STRAP

SEAT

CANTLE

CHEYENNE ROLL

SKIRT

JOCKEY

GIRTH IS UNDER HERE

SADDLE STRINGS ARE USED FOR TYING A BED ROLL AND SADDLE BAGS TO THE SADDLE

COWBOYS TIE THIS STRAP CALLED A FLANK CINCH UNDER THE HORSE'S BELLY. IT HELPS TO KEEP THE SADDLE IN PLACE FOR ROPING

STIRRUP

A STRAP IS TIED TIGHTLY ROUND THE HORSE JUST IN FRONT OF ITS HIND LEGS. THE HORSE KICKS AND BUCKS TO TRY AND GET RID OF THE STRAP.

A JUDGE IN THE ARENA USES SPECIAL SIGNALS TO GIVE MARKS TO BOTH THE HORSE AND THE RIDER.

Sometimes the calf is thrown to the ground as the horse stops and the rope pulls tight round its neck. Sometimes the cowboy picks up the calf and drops it on its side. He carries a piece of rope in his mouth, called pigging string, to tie up the calf's feet.

As soon as the calf is lying on the ground with its legs tied, the cowboy raises his arms, and the judges record the time. The winners of these competitions can sometimes lasso a calf, dismount, throw the calf to the ground and tie it up in less than 12 seconds.

Index

Arabs	3,4-5,16,28	war	8-9
		working	10-11
battles	8,9	horse transport	6-7
bronco riding	30-31	hunters	17
breeds of horses	4-5,28-29	hunting	23
cavalry	8-9,20	Lipizzaners	5,28-29
coaching	6-7		
cobs	17	Olympic Games	
cross-country events	20-21		12-13,14-15,18,19,20-21
dressage	18-19,20	paces, changing	18,19
driving	16,22	piaffe	18,29
		pirouette	19,29
European Championships	15,21	polo	23
eventing	20-21	prehistoric horses	2-3
feeding	24-25,26	racing	26-27
fences	15,20,21	racing stables	24-25
		ranching	11
Grand National	23	rodeo	30-31
		rugs	13,21,27
Hacks	17		
Hackneys	16	showing	16-17
harness, parts of	7	show jumping	12-13,14-15,21
horses,		steeplechasing	20,23
action	16,17		
breeds of	4-5	tack	13,16,24
conformation	16		
domestication	2-3	war horses	8-9
history of	2-3	weighing in	21,26,27
prehistoric	2-3	working horses	10-11

© Usborne Publishing Ltd 1978

First published in 1978
Usborne Publishing Ltd
20 Garrick Street
London WC2 9BJ

Published in Australia by
Rigby Ltd
Adelaide, Sydney, Melbourne,
Brisbane, Perth.

Published in Canada by
Hayes Publishing Ltd,
Burlington, Ontario

Printed in Spain by
Printer, industria gráfica sa
Tuset, 19   Barcelona
D. L. B. 46469-1977

Photographs: p.12/13 E.D. Lacey; p.14/15 E.D. Lacey; p.16/17 Bob Langrish; p.10 Whitbread & Co Ltd; p.11 United States Travel Service; p.18 (top) Bob Langrish, (lower) Werner Ernst; p.19 (top left) van der Slikke, (top right) Bob Langrish, (lower left) Bob Langrish, (lower right) E.D. Lacey; p.20/21 E.D. Lacey; p.22 (top) Bob Langrish, (lower left) Bob Langrish, (lower right) Peter Roberts; p.23 (top left, right) Jim Meads, (lower) Peter Roberts; p.24/25 Fiona Vigors Ltd; p.26 Colorlabs International; p.27 (top) Racing Information Bureau, (lower) Wallis Photographers; p.28/29 Film-und Lichtbildstelle des Bundesministeriums fur Land-und Forstwirtschaft, Wien.